Five (and a bit) Days in the Life of

Also by Val Bird and illustrated by
Rebecca Cundy

A Birthday in the Life of Ozzie Kingsford

Five (and a bit) Days in the Life of

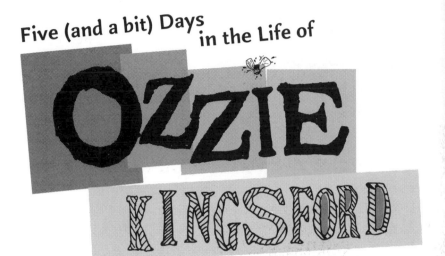

OZZIE

KINGSFORD

Val Bird

**ILLUSTRATED BY
REBECCA CUNDY**

RANDOM HOUSE
NEW ZEALAND

A RANDOM HOUSE BOOK published by Random House New Zealand
18 Poland Road, Glenfield, Auckland, New Zealand

For more information about our titles go to www.randomhouse.co.nz

A catalogue record for this book is available from the National Library
of New Zealand

First published 2008

ISBN 978 1 86979 053 0

Random House New Zealand uses non chlorine-bleached papers from
sustainably managed plantation forests

Design: Anna Seabrook
Illustrations: Rebecca Cundy

Printed in Australia by Griffin Press

The Kingsford family is ever so chuffed to dedicate this book to Ros Bird and Troy Cundy, and also applaud them on their impressive choice of respective marriage partners.

THE BEGINNING

Today is Wednesday the 12th of December, which is eleven days after my eleventh birthday.
Weather: it's a bit cloudy.

The time is 6.35 pm — my family is sitting around the dining room table eating our un-delicious tea.

How to make an un-delicious tea:
1 Open the fridge door.
2 Grab any old leftover stuff.

3 Wipe off any yuck-spots-of-mould.
4 Chuck all the bits and pieces in a hotted-up pan.
5 Stir-fry until sort-of cooked through.
6 Slop a big spoonful on starving person's plate.

7 Give the stuff a fancy name such as Surprise Mixed Delights.
8 Then command, "EAT YOUR DELIGHTS, OR YOU WILL BE IN TROUBLE."

The food tastes really yuck.

I'm thinking of having a serious food rebellion when the phone rings. As usual Mum answers it.

Dad reckons: "Your mother likes to answer the phone because she possesses sneaky tendencies, and likes to check up on incoming calls." Which he insists is a "breach of our personal rights". He said this after he missed playing in the Hideous Hitters' Golf Tournament at Taupo — that was when Mum forgot to pass on the invitation-to-come-and-play telephone message.

In this case, when she places the phone to her ear, her face breaks out in a great big

smile. Then she goes into the next room and shuts the door.

"Mmm," says Dad, "your mother looks like the cat that got the bowl of whipped cream. I wonder who she's talking to."

"I reckon that looks like a beloved person smile," I tell him, while taking the opportunity to feed our devoted dog Snoops the remains of my tea. We are FORTUNATE that our dog is a hairy

walking garbage-disposal unit, and eats most things including Mum's cooking failures.

UNFORTUNATELY my sister Holly, whose nickname is **The Brat** spots me.

"AHHH! I'll tell Mum on you!" she

screeches. "Nobody is allowed to feed Snoops at the table — you're breaking the rules and you'll get into the BIGGEST-EVER trouble!"

Then Dad says, "Well Holly, in that case you'll have to tell on me too," and he gives Snoops the un-delicious leftovers from his plate, "but I don't think telling tales is a good idea!" He points a finger at her . . .

FACT When Dad points a finger, it means he's issuing a serious warning.

FORTUNATELY, Snoops gobbles evidence of the mealtime mutiny before Mum comes bursting back into the room.

"That was my brother Rusty, who is **your Uncle**," she declares in an excited voice, while looking directly at my sister and me.

"He's been to a conference in Sydney, and before he heads back to London, he's coming **to see us**. He'll be here **this Saturday** . . . and he wants

us to invite the rest of the family **around for tea**."

She pauses for a moment and her eyes go all misty like she's going to cry.

"Do you realise it's over **ten** years since I last saw him?"

The fact that my hard-working, school-teachery mother has not seen her beloved brother for such a long time means nothing to my golf-nutter Dad. I watch him as the *no-golf-this-weekend* shock waves begin to roll in — and seeing he has not had a game of golf since before he lost his glasses, the shock is tremendously colossal.

His bottom jaw drops, his eyes fill with self-pity.

Then a flash of horrible-horror hurtles across his face . . .

And I'm sure I see his beard quiver as reality sets in:

A He's just picked up his new glasses from the optometrist.

B He's ready for golf action.

C But instead Mum's family will be coming to visit.

D Mum will put on her bossy britches.

E Dad will have to do this-that-and-the-other-thing.

■ 14

Prediction: This forthcoming social event will throw my parents into a state of pre-visitor tension, and our household will suffer from DISHARMONY.

I check the time on my new multi-functional, solar-powered wicked watch (that Mum and Dad bought me for my birthday) and it reads twenty-five minutes to eight o'clock when we get down to organising Uncle Rusty's visit.

Mum takes a seat at the head of the table and says in a General Manager's voice, "Rusty will be picking up a rental car from Auckland airport, and should arrive here mid-afternoon Saturday. He will stay for two nights but has to head back to Auckland early on Monday morning." She gives us a beaming smile, "We **must** be organised and show him what an efficient, well-adjusted family unit we are."

Then she looks in my direction.

"In the spirit of cooperation I will call out the names and Ozzie, you can write a guest list, and please use your best printing. I don't want any of your *Scruffy writing*, which nobody can read."

The Brat squawks, "I want to write the list."

But when I (har! har!) cunningly point out how late it is, Mum says . . . "Oh, my goodness, I didn't realise it was **that** late. Holly, go and have your shower, and then it's off to bed."

"But I'll be eight years old soon," she protests, "I can stay up for longer. EVERYBODY in my class at school is allowed to stay up waywayway past midnight."

"I don't care what your school friends do," Mum says, in a firm not-to-be-argued-with voice, "you will do exactly what you are told. Now go!"

The Brat gives Mum a drop-dead look, but knowing she is defeated step-by-slow-step sniffles her way out of the room . . . while Dad, who looks depressed, picks up the newspaper and browses through the "cars for sale" section — our station wagon is looking a bit tatty after Dad dropped it in a ditch. I pick up my pen and write:

This is the Official Invitation List for Uncle Rusty's visit. as written by:

Ozzie Devon Kingsford

that's me

Who is the great-great-great-great grandson of a world famous explorer.

One: Gramma Grace. *← Boring*

Two: Granddad Pete. *← Boring*

Three: Great-Aunt Emma. *← Boring*

Four, Five, Six, Seven, and Eight: Aunt Nellie and Uncle Andy. *Boring! x3*

And my boring cousins:

Gavin the Geeky Gawker. *Geek#1*

William the Geeky Wimp. *Geek#2*

Miriam the Geeky Mouse. *Geek#3*

Nine: Nigel Bothersome (Rusty's old school friend). *← also Boring!*

Ten: His wife Patty Bothersome.

Eleven: Rusty who is the guest of honour.

Then us lot: Mum, Dad, me and The Brat.

That makes fifteen — but I reckon we should count our dog, Snoops, (whose pedigree name is "Highland Bonnie Prince Charles XVII of Winchester on Brown Rye") who likes to sleep under the table at family gatherings.

"That makes sixteen in total," I state using my official counting voice.

Mum frowns, like she does when she's thinking hard and waves her finger in the air. "What about inviting . . ."

But she never gets a chance to finish because Dad appears from behind his newspaper and orders, "That's enough!"

I get in quick . . . "**Pleasssseeee** can I invite Fletch?"

(Fletch Jessup is my mate.)

"Of course you can," says Mum, "Fletch is considered one of the family."

"And he's not a Hot-Head," Dad adds.

HONORARY KINGSFORD

Red hair is the predominant gene in our family.

Using my advanced mathematical skills I add up the guest list and find we have:

! HOTHEAD

8 red heads (including Mum, The Brat and me).

3 blackish/brown heads (that includes our Dad and Snoops).

3 old greys.

2 unknown Bothersomes.

AND 1 one blondish Fletch.

Ozzie Rulz!

Holly is a pain!

Fletch eats worms

I tell Dad, "Inviting Fletch swings the genetic balance — we have EIGHT Hot-Heads, and NINE multi-coloureds."

"Hooray!" Dad gloats. "Ozzie, do you realise that due to our united efforts, we've avoided a Hot-Head takeover bid, and one day the free world will thank us for it!"

Mum tosses him a hostile look but Dad just gives a silly smirk and then starts chuckling to himself.

I'm lying in bed reading an article in *The Weirdo Weekly Wag* magazine. There's an interesting bit about forestry workers who reckon the forest sprites (otherwise known as mischievous forest dwellers), have been playing practical jokes . . .

"I'm sure it was those little blighters that stuck my lunch box up a tree — I'm climbing up to get it back when I hear this laughing noise, then when I open it up I discover somebody or something's made off with me slab of fruit cake!"

"I only took my boots off while we were having a cuppa, and then bingo — they're gone, never to be seen again."

I'm wondering if sprites really do eat fruit cake, and how a little sprite could make off with a big pair of boots, when Mum comes into my bedroom.

She sits on the side of my bed and says in a tender voice, "Do you realise you were only five months old when your Uncle Rusty last saw you. Oh! You were such a cute little fellah."

She does a little sniff — sniff, which means she is getting a bit emotional.

"Rusty has never even seen Holly."

"BOY! He doesn't know how lucky he is," I say in a philosophical tone of voice. "And speaking as a responsible citizen, I reckon you should send him an email warning him of the possible outcome of meeting her — but then again — (har! har!) we might scare him off, and he will decide to stay away!"

Mum laughs as well, "Har! Har! Har!"

And then reaches out a hand and ruffles my hair.

"Ozzie, although you may not realise it, deep down inside you really do care about

your sister," she says in a soppy tone of voice.

"I dunno about that!" I protest.

"We all know Holly can be testing," Mum confides, "but you must remember that children of her age are naturally chaotic." Then she leans forward and points to where her heart should be, and says in a hush-hush tone of voice, "She's not a child that shows her true feelings, but I know that deep down inside she secretly loves you!"

As Mum speaks those very words there comes a cry in the night . . .

" YUCKY-OOO, I DON'T love Ozzie. YUCK MUM, you shouldn't say things like that! Nobody in the whole world loves Ozzie! He's a YUCKY-OOO POOH Dummy-BUMMY!"

"HOLLY!" Mum shouts in her most EXASPERATED voice, "What are you doing sneaking up on us — you're supposed to be fast asleep! And how many times do I have to tell you, stop calling people 'dummy-bummy'!"

The Brat goes running off down the

hallway with Mum in hot pursuit.

Snoops decides this is a perfect time to play **action dog** — he leap-bounds off the end of my bed and, switching into super-speed-mode, chases Mum.

I hear **The Brat** squawk, "You can't catch me!"

Then Dad yells, "What the heck is going on!"

Next a door bangs shut . . . BANG!

The BANG is followed by a loud CRASH as some unfortunate object falls to the floor. I hear Mum wail, "oh no"

For one second there's an ominous silence . . .

Then once again the action starts — next comes the sound of galloping paws as Snoops runs back up the hallway . . . does a sharp right turn into my bedroom; leaps on to my bed, dives under the duvet cover and gives a series of whispery-whimpers. I'm just giving Snoops some calming pats, when The Brat also comes galloping down the hallway, turns a sharp right into my bedroom, and, while warning me, "Don't you tell Mum!", she opens my wardrobe door and goes into hiding. I roll my eyes — that's just what I need . . . A Brat in my wardrobe!

 Those forest workers have got it easy — I reckon my sister's more trouble than a whole army of forest sprites!

 I still reckon Mum should send a Brat-warning email to Uncle Rusty!

From: thekingsfordfamily@goosemail.co.nz
To: rusty@theworldbankinvestmentplanner@moneymail.co.uk

After due thought and consideration we feel it only fair to warn you that young **Holly** has many **undesirable** screwball qualities due to the fact she was born when the moon was full (for further information on the subject see the thirteenth edition of *The Weirdo Weekly Wag*). However, we are delighted to inform you that young **Ozzie** (who was born when the moon was on the wane) is of **stable character** and has proved to be an **upstanding** member of the community and is deserving of the **many gifts** I'm sure you will bring. Lots of love, and looking forward to seeing you soon...

your sister Trish.

p.s. find a recent photo of The Brat attached.

 our_least_loved_child.jpg

THE HARDEST-
WORKING BIT

Today is Thursday the 13th of December.
Weather: some sun, some cloud.

After a mind-numbing day of listening
to educational propaganda, I walk home
from school with Fletch. I tell him about
Uncle Rusty coming to visit and ask him if he
can come on Saturday.

He says, "Yeah, sure thing."

"That's cool," I tell him, "but I feel it's
my duty to warn you my cousins are strictly
geeks."

"How come I haven't met that lot before?" Fletch asks.

"They only arrived back from the United States a couple of months ago," I explain. "According to Mum, Uncle Andy is a Highly-Respected-Scientific-Big-Wig and we're lucky to have him back in New Zealand."

"What sort of work does he do?" Fletch questions.

"I dunno," I say. "It's all brain-boggling stuff, but Dad reckons he's a professional know-it-all nutter."

Fletch looks thoughtful, "Will I be the only one who's not a relative?"

"Not quite," I say. "But it doesn't matter, Mum and Dad always say that you're part of our family."

"Do they really say that?" he says with a happy look on his face.

"Yeah — fair dinkum."

"That's REVOLUTIONARY," he declares, and then scratches his head and asks, "What does your Rusty Old Uncle do in England?"

"He's an investment manager with an international bank," I tell him.

"That must be electrifying stuff," says Fletch in a droll voice. "Perhaps he could give us some hints on investing our pocket money."

It's spot-on fourteen minutes after three o'clock when I say goodbye to Fletch and turn up the driveway to my house. As usual Snoops is waiting out by the gate for me. When he sees me his eyes light up, his body wriggles with excitement and he calls out: "Ruff-Wuff-Wuff."

This in doggy language means: I'm overjoyed, excited and thrilled to see you.

Once the wag-tail welcoming ritual is over, and he's had a million-and-a-half pats, Snoops and I wander into the kitchen to find Mum has an assortment of recipe books strewn all over the table. She is glaring at them with passionate intent.

I call out to her, "Hey Mum, Fletch says he can come on Saturday."

Without thinking she automatically says, "That's good." Then realising she has a victim within her grasp . . . she puts her hands on her hips and gets ready to boss me around.

"I want you to get changed and then go and mow the lawns."

"They don't need mowing," I protest, "I just did them the other day."

"That was Sunday, it is now Thursday, and the weather forecast is for rain tomorrow, and

I have other plans for you on Saturday — so you'd better mow them now! We don't want the lawns to look untidy for our visitors DO WE?" And with those words my fate is sealed — nobody in this whole world argues with my mother when she says DO WE in that particular tone of voice.

I've changed my clothes and am on my way to get the mower out of the shed, when Mum puts her head out of the window and yells out . . . "I want you to do the lawns PROPERLY, no racing around at rocket speed and missing bits."

The Brat pokes her head out of her bedroom window; she's eating a chocolate-coated ice cream, she licks her lips and then pokes her ice cream-coated tongue out at me!

Gggggggrrrrrrr I feel a rush of anger roar through my inner system — how come she gets a treat after breaking Mum's heirloom vase while I get all the jobs to do? But I stay calm and cool on the outside and pretend I don't see her!

That will miff her off — har! har!

Our lawn mower is positively prehistoric. It takes me fifteen vigorous pull-pull-pulls of the cord before it slowly putt-putt-putters into action. I keep telling Dad that if he doesn't buy a new mower soon, one day my arm might FALL OFF.

I point out to him what the headlines in the local paper would say:

Kingsford County Daily News

POPULAR LOCAL IDENTITY LOSES ARM

BECAUSE FATHER WAS TOO <u>STINGY</u> TO BUY A NEW MOTOR MOWER

But seeing it's MY job to mow the lawns, I don't think HE cares.

FACT IT WOULD BE A DIFFERENT STORY IF **HE** HAD TO PULL THE CORD!

I reckon it's a possible case of **JUVENILE SLAVE LABOUR** — just in case a representative from the United Nations Child Protection Foundation comes to town, I've made a note on page forty-three of my personal journal regarding this issue.

We have pizza and salad for tea.

Mum says she nearly suffered a dose of extreme EXASPERATION trying to make up her mind what to have for tea on Saturday night. Now she has put all the recipe books back in the cupboard apart from one, which is titled: *Delicious Summer Outdoor Meals to Impress the Fussiest Guest.*

"I've come to a decision," she says. "The weatherman says the rain will have cleared by

Saturday, so we'll have a barbecue meal." She gives a satisfied sigh, "And at least that way I'm relieved of cooking duties." She gives Dad a meaningful look . . .

The shock-wave hits and Dad just manages to contain a large protest-splutter.

Our dad is not one of those dads that gets a sense of accomplishment from cooking on the barbecue — to him food is something that appears miraculously from the depths of Mum's kitchen.

Mum turns to Dad, "Will you check the barbecue gas bottle?"

He swallows hard and puts a false smile on his face and says, "Yes, dear."

"And I'd appreciate it if you'd water blast the courtyard."

Dad false-smiles and says, "Yes, dear," again.

"And on Saturday morning, you and Holly can go to Very Berry Land and pick some strawberries, then to the Free-Range Farm for a tray of eggs, and on your way home grab some fresh vegetables from the market."

Dad nods his head and says another, "Yes, dear."

Then Mum says, "Everybody on the guest list says they can come."

Dad rolls his eyes and says, "That's nice, dear."

Then she turns to me, "Ozzie, your bedroom is awfully messy. I want you to tidy it up before you go to bed tonight — and tomorrow after school I want you to sweep out the garage."

I bow my head and say in my best oriental voice, "Ahhh! Yes, dear. Ahhh! Yes, dear. Your honourable slave both hears and obeys."

Fatherly Reaction: he goes, HAR! HAR! HAR! NICE ONE OZZIE!

Motherly Reaction: she gives both Dad and me a practised scowl and suggests we zip our lips; otherwise she'll serve us a large slab of humble pie. (For further information on this subject, Google "eat humble pie".)

Before I have my shower and get ready for bed, I do what I'm told and tidy up my room. I (har! har!) pick up all the things off the floor and any other messy objects within reach and dump them in the bottom of my

wardrobe. According to my watch . . . the whole process takes me **three** minutes and **forty** seconds — this gives me an **overall energy-saving, efficiency rating** of 97.5 (that is according to *The Weirdo Good Housekeeping Guide*).

Snoops and I get into bed, he's already snoring, and I'm reading another attention-grabbing article in the latest *The Weirdo Weekly Wag* which explores the possibility of a (so far) undiscovered, undersea world off the coast of Stewart Island, which is said to be inhabited by web-footed human-like creatures, when Mum comes into my room.

She looks about, her eyes darting quickly from here to there.

"It didn't take you long to tidy up your room," she states in a mistrustful tone of voice.

I give my Boy Scout salute. "I am an

efficient room-tidying machine," I tell her, "and it's only due to my modesty that I've never informed you that I graduated from *The Weirdo Weekly Wag* anti-messiness training course with *Supreme Honours*."

But my words fail to convince her; and I see a disbelieving dart shoot out of her left eye. Then, without further discussion, she walks towards the wardrobe door, and **opens** it.

"Ozzie Devon Kingsford," she shrieks, "you are a LYING little toad!"

To preserve my reputation, I will not go into details regarding the further consequences of the sight that greeted her, other than to say she threw a right snot-faced wobbly and marched out of the room with my *Weirdo* magazine tucked under her arm.

WET, WET AND WETTER

Today is Friday the 14th of December, which would have been Black Friday if it was the 13th. **Weather: it's raining.**

Mum wakes me up at 6 am so I will have time to get my room tided up PROPERLY before I go to school. **And then** she says, "There was a phone call last night from Fletch's mother, and Fletch will be coming to stay the weekend because his parents have to go to Wellington urgently."

"Why?" I ask.

"Nana Jessup's in hospital," she says in a sad tone of voice, "she had a car accident."

Fletch and I walk home from school together.

It's raining hard, and water is running down the gutters.

Fletch tells me that his parents are hoping to bring his Nana back with them.

"She will need someone to look after her," he says.

"What sort of crash was it?" I ask.

"Dunno really," he says, "but she's got a reputation as a scatterbrained driver; Mum reckons she can't understand how she ever passed her drivers' test in the first place."

It is 3.35 pm when we walk up our driveway.

Snoops, our faithful Highland Terrier, is waiting for us by the back door, but we don't get time for the usual greeting ritual because Mum opens the door, and we find she is in a state of EXTREME exasperation.

"Don't come in here," she yells, "the dishwasher's flooded the kitchen — I want you to go into the garage and get some buckets and sponge mops — you boys are going to have to be the water-mopper-uppers because I've got to go and pick up Holly from Buzzy Bee Club and then go to the supermarket."

Please take note — my mother did not say *hello* to us.

She did not ask — have you had a nice day?

But worst of all, she did not say *please* would you mop up the floor.

■■◤

It is 4.55 pm when Mum gets home with my juvenile delinquent sister.

The Brat is wearing her Buzzy Bee Antennas and looks like a **real** twit-let.

Mum looks at the kitchen floor and says, "Thank you boys, you've done a great job." She hands us a Groovy Fudge Chocolate Bar, "And here's something to give you an energy boost before you tackle sweeping out the garage."

Dad brings home fish and chips for tea. Mum calls us in from the garage, where Fletch and I have been hiding out (in case Mum finds any more jobs for us). After washing our hands and then being sent back to re-wash them, we finally pass hygiene inspection and sit around the table with Mum, Dad and The Brat and eat the fish and chips out of the newspaper. Dad smacks The Brat's hand for being greedy and stuffing too many chips in her mouth at once. "Don't be a piggy," he grumbles at her. "Mind your manners."

Har! Har!

The Brat screws up her eyes and glares at him, but Dad acts as if he doesn't notice.

After Mum tells Dad all about the naughty-floor-flooding-dishwasher, and how she simply has to have a new well-behaved one, she gives a worried look, "I thought the rain would've cleared up by now," she says while waving a chip in the air, "I hope the weatherman has got it right."

"We had the radio going when we were in the garage," I announce in my official news-casters voice, "and they said something about a heavy rain warning."

Mum's eyes open wide, "You're pulling my leg . . . they didn't?"

"Yes, they did," I dispute. "Fletch heard it TOO!"

"Yeah," says Fletch, "they said the front has become stationary and we can expect 120 millimetres of rain in the next 24 hours."

■■◣

After tea Mum goes back to the supermarket to get some different types of food in case it is too wet tomorrow to have a barbecue. The Brat gets to go with her. Dad is landed with the job of emptying out the dishwasher and seeing if he can figure out why it flooded the kitchen. Fletch and I are just going to sneak off to watch *The Daring Desert Daredevils* on television . . . when Dad calls out, "You boys come here."

"What FOR?" I question, poking my

head around the doorway.

"These dishes are still dirty," Dad proclaims. "And I've just volunteered you and Fletch to wash and dry them, and when you've finished, then I'll have a look at the dishwasher."

"But, but, but . . ." I protest, "we've **already** mopped the kitchen floor **and** swept out the garage."

"Oh dear," says Dad in a sarcastic tone of voice, "you poor little things must be **all worn out** — never mind, after you've done the dishes you can go straight to bed and get some well-deserved rest."

I have a final rally-up for fair treatment!

"Are you going to help us?"

"Not enough room in the kitchen for all of us," he states in a bossy voice, "I'll just have a look at the golf on the TV while I'm waiting for you to finish."

FACT Sometimes my father can be unfeeling, pitiless and self-absorbed.

Possible FACT I have been born into a life of domestic drudgery.

We unload a large-huge-humungous amount of dishes out of the dishwasher on bench. I run the water and squirt the guaranteed-to-save-our-world eco-dishwashing liquid into the water — I wash and Fletch dries.

He flick-flicks the tea towel at my bare leg and says, "I guess this is what you meant when you said I was considered part of the family — and while it's a privilege to have two families, you didn't tell me your folks were running a **slave labour camp**."

We both roll eyes at each other, and burst into hoots of laughter.

■■◣

As usual when Fletch comes to stay we are sharing my bedroom.

Fletch is sleeping in the comfy camp fold-up bed, which has been set up against

the wall. I'm in my bed, which is under the window.

 Snoops is curled up on the end of Fletch's bed.

 Snoops ALWAYS sleeps on MY bed.

Question: Does Snoops like Fletch more than he likes me?

Another question: Or is this a novelty event?

A last question: Perhaps Snoops thinks that Fletch needs company?

A very last question: Or is Snoops trying to tell me something, and if so, what?

I shake my head, there are too many questions revolving around and I don't know the answer to any of them . . . and the rain is pelting down something awful.

And then in the back of my confused brain I hear it . . . Har! Har! Har! Har! It's the sound of rascally laughter.

I hear the wind roar with destructive rage as it tries to force open the window.

My body turns hot and then cold — they've come back again!

 It's the sound of those annoying forest sprites — the ones that caused such problems on my birthday — perhaps the very same ones that play practical jokes on the forest workers? Fletch and I had already figured they'd followed us home, but I'd hoped they had moved on and found someone else to annoy.

"Can you hear what I hear?" I whisper to Fletch.

"Yeah!" he whispers back. "It's them, isn't it."

"You've got it right! I looked them up on the Internet — and it said they've been known to bond with certain people, and even stay with them for the rest of their living days!" (For further information on this subject, Google "forest sprites".)

"Critical stuff," says Fletch in a serious whispering tone of voice — "I can only hope it's you they're attached to and not me!"

 Why do we feel the need to whisper?

Question: Do forest sprites have big ears?

RAINING CATS AND DOGS

The first bit of this day, Saturday the 15th of December, which is the date that Uncle Rusty arrives.
Weather: it is raining.

Mum wakes Fletch and me up at 7.30 am and, using a bossy tone of voice, informs us: "The last sitting for breakfast will be at eight o'clock, so if you are not seated by then, you miss out."

"Radical stuff," says Fletch, "and I think she means it!"

"Helpers! I hope Uncle Rusty is worth all this trouble," I say.

■■◣

My watch tells me it is exactly a quarter to eight when Fletch and I take our seats at the table for breakfast.

Our mum is beside herself with a dose of organisational EXASPERATION!

"How dare it rain!" she shouts to no one in particular. "We are going to have to have an indoor meal. It's not fair — it would have been lovely outdoors . . . the garden is looking so beautiful!"

Dad turns on the radio for the eight o'clock news and the announcer says:

"*Central North Island has been thrown into a state of chaos due to flooding. State Highway*

One is blocked in three places and the public are advised to stay home and leave the car safely in the garage . . . and the weather forecasters say . . . the worst could still be to come!"

"Oh my giddiness," says Mum, "I hope Rusty gets through."

As Mum says those words **The Brat** walks into the kitchen. She is wearing her pink Teddy Bear shorty pyjamas, her hair is sticking up like a scarecrow and she is yawning and rubbing her eyes at the same time.

"Hello sleepyhead," says Dad, "having trouble waking up are you?"

"YES — cos I got WOKEN UP when it was dark and I HAD to talk to Uncle

Rusty." The Brat snivels, and then gives another big yawn.

"Did you have a dream you were talking to him?" Mum asks.

"No!" The Brat says, **"I really DID** talk to him on the telephone."

Mum and Dad shoot each other a surprised look . . .

"Are you sure you weren't dreaming?" Mum asks in a gentle probing voice.

"NO," The Brat insists, "you were all asleep and I heard the phone and I answered it and it was Uncle Rusty . . . and he said, HELLO Holly are your Mum and Dad there . . . and I said that you were asleep and he said . . . okay can you tell them something when they wake up?"

"And?" questions Mum.

Holly folds her arms, and looks very important before finally spitting the words out. "He said, to tell you, he got fogged-up and he's running late."

"Did he say anything else?" Dad urges.

She shakes her head, and then reconsiders . . .

"He said he was On the plane, and the pilot-man said to turn Off all the phones, so nobody will be able to ring him."

"How come we didn't hear the phone ring?" Mum ponders.

Dad goes, "Mmm, good question," and then goes off to check their bedroom connection . . . and comes back shaking his head . . .

"The phone in our bedroom was unplugged," he tells Mum.

"Oh no!" she says, "I forgot! I unplugged it

the other day because it kept tinkling." Then she turns to Holly, "Do you know what time it was when Rusty rang up?"

"No!" she announces. "If you want me to tell the time, then you have to buy me a watch like Ozzie has."

■■◣

It is now 9.35 am.

Dad is taking The Brat with him to do the shopping.

Seeing it is so wet Mum says he doesn't have to pick fresh strawberries, he is allowed to buy some from the vegetable shop — and on his way Dad will drop Fletch off at the school for Saturday band practice. I figure I can tag along and go to band practice with Fletch, but Mum thinks otherwise.

"I'm going to make dinky individual custard pies, plus Fairy-Delish-Delight passionfruit pudding with chocolate meringue and layers of whipped cream — and you . . ." she reaches out a hand and ruffles my hair, "are going to stay home and do the vacuum cleaning."

I put a pitiful look on my face and complain.

"Oh MUM! You're being seriously irrational! Vacuum cleaning is a GIRLS' job — do you realise if I'm even spotted from a distance it'll wreck my manly reputation."

Mum gives me a disapproving look and

says, "Ozzie, you should rethink your attitude, and instead count your blessings that you've been born into an **equal opportunity household**, which means we don't **discriminate** between male and female."

Just in case of **sneaky-prying** eyes, I pull the curtains while I vacuum the lounge and only get as far as vacuuming the first bit of the hallway, when Mum flicks my switch and the cleaner turns itself off . . .

"What did you do that for?" I question.

"I need you to go next door to Missus Hobbs and ask if I can borrow her electric beater, mine has broken down," she grumps in an EXASPERATED tone of voice, "I've got all the ingredients on the bench, the egg whites are half beaten and now no mixer." She waves a hand in the air, "This day is turning into an absolute nightmare!"

"Why can't YOU go to Missus Hobbs?" I ask.

"I don't want to get my hair wet, or even damp for that matter," she says, "It took me simply ages to do it this morning." To bring home the point she pit-pats the side of her fuzzy red hair with her right hand.

I weigh up the situation.

 It's awfully wet outside.

Another FACT If I go out there I could get —
- **A** Very wet.
- **B** Very, very wet.
- **C** Totally saturated. Or,
- **D** Possibly drowned.

As (at this moment in time) I wish to remain dry, I then carry out an intelligent assessment of the situation, and come up with what I consider a flawless piece of reasoning as to: why Mum should go out in the wet, while I stay home and keep dry.

I look sombrely at my mother, and then put on my Ultimate Defense Attorney voice: "Dear Madam Kingsford," I declare, "after referring to the court records . . . I feel it's MY DUTY to remind you, it's been recently acknowledged that this is an EQUAL OPPORTUNITY HOUSEHOLD!" I point to the back

door. "And what about MY hair getting wet? Have you taken into consideration the fact that I also spent simply ages, if not half a century, doing it this morning?"

huMPH! Grumble and grump . . . and one more grumble for good measure.

My cunning **stay-dry** EQUAL OPPORTUNITY strategy did not work and I find myself trudging about in the POURING rain.

I walk up Missus Hobbs' driveway, and knock on her door, only to find there is no answer. I say a mild bleep word to myself (a bleep word = an unacceptable word) and go to check if her car is in the garage — this is to make sure Missus Hobbs has really gone out and is not lying inside the house injured and unable to call for help — my mother says it's **important** to check on her as she lives by herself.

I am getting wetter and wetter by the half-second. I look through the side window of the garage and find her car is gone. I turn and start walking back towards our house when Cougar comes running out of the cat flap to see me . . .

"**Weooow . . . ooowww . . . weooowww!**" he cries.

Which I figure in cat language means: *Hello Ozzie, it's real nice of you to drop by to see me, my owner has gone out and I am lonely.*

Cougar is Missus Hobbs' oversized, ginger moggy.

 Missus Hobbs loves Cougar — she calls him, "My **lovee wee**, furry baby." And while he's very sociable, he's also mischievous and considered a neighbourhood troublemaker of the Grade Six variety . . . in comparison **The Brat** is a Grade Ten (which is top of the pops).

I give him a pat, and he is so happy he whirls himself around my legs and turns his purr-motor on to full bore. "Good wild cat," I tell him, and he purrs even louder.

 FACT Cougar has a purr that sounds like a large lion.

After a minute or two, I say goodbye and head back for home.

But Cougar wants to come too.

He follows me down his driveway, and then turns up our driveway.

I stop and order: "GO HOME, Cougar."

But he just runs up to me and starts whirling around my legs.

I pick him up and take him back to his driveway; I put him down on the ground and then point my finger in the direction of his home and shout: "GO HOME,

COUGAR." And then I turn and run as fast as I can back to our house.

But Cougar doesn't want to go home.

He turns back and starts running after me.

In fact he runs so fast that within seconds he is right up beside me.

I dash up the steps to our back door, and he starts whirling around my legs AGAIN.

"You dumbest-ever-wet-cat," I tell him, "YOU GO HOME!"

I take off my raincoat and gumboots, and then I open the back door and make a dive for a cat-free environment, but Cougar has no intention of letting me escape.

The pesky moggy dashes through the door.

"Weooow...oOwWWw...weeoOwWWW!"

he cries as he announces his arrival.

THOUGHT Seeing as there's a dedicated, cat-chasing, Highland terrier in residence, this is a really dumb thing to do!

Then a big gust of wind grabs hold of the

door and slams it shut . . . BANG!

The **BANG** gives Cougar a fright
and he puts his fur up — at
the same time I make
a mad-dash to

scoop him up (so I can chuck him out the door), and I just manage to grab hold of him when I hear an unwelcome noise: "Ruff — Wuff — Ruff — Wuff."

And here comes Snoops.

RUFF
WUFF
RUFF
WUFF

His pink tongue is hanging out, his eyes wide open with cat-chasing passion, and his little paws are travelling at a new world record speed of a million-and-a-half kilometres per second. Cougar immediately decides he has made a mistake by coming visiting.

He digs his claws into my arm . . .

I cry

"ouch OUCH

-OOOOOOUCH!

Cougar goes **HiSSssssss** and, taking advantage of my critically wounded state, departs my arms and takes off into space.

 Cougar lands on Mum's kitchen workbench, amid all the pudding ingredients — Snoops does an extra loud "RUFF, RUFF, WOOF, RUFF," then not slowing down and using a kitchen chair as a launching pad, he hi-flies through the air in pursuit of the visiting moggy.

UNFORTUNATELY Snoops also lands on Mum's kitchen workbench, but his Anti-lock Braking System is dog-gone faulty. As a result, his hairy body skids/slides along the bench, knocking over the ingredients for

the delicious puddings. There is a series of loud CRASHES and BANGS as mixing bowls and assorted kitchen cooking equipment slither about before crashing to the floor. The custard stuff dribbles down the cupboard doors, and there's a big chocolate egg-white puddle spreading over the kitchen floor. Cougar is now in full flight and skittles Mum's collection of herbs and spices, her prized sugar bowl and matching milk jug . . . and finally, after making a mighty leap, ends up taking refuge on top of the fridge.

UNFORTUNATELY on top of the fridge is where my mother has put her favourite potted plant with pink flowers, which, after being knocked over by Cougar, teeters for all of one-fiftieth of a second before yielding to its fate and also splattering to the floor.

The potting mix splatters about like a black dirt-bomb, and at this moment, my stomach sinks to the bottom of my toes, my heart goes BOOM — BOOM — BOOM as a state of pure panic sets in — for a tick-of-time I consider fleeing the scene, but before I get the chance I hear another unwelcome noise.

 it's my mother who comes running into the kitchen flapping her arms like an old mother chook and squawking in a loud voice:

"WHAT THE BLEEPY — BLEEP IS GOING ON IN HERE!"

FACT This could be described as a cat-astrophic situation. (For further information on this subject, Google "dog chase cat".)

Things may well have turned out a teeny bit better, if my father and The Brat had taken a little longer to do the shopping. But having arrived home, they pick this very moment of time to open the back door. Cougar, seeing the chance of escape, decides it's time for him to go back where he belongs — he cat-leaps down from the top of the fridge and makes a mad-moggy dash for the door.

UNFORTUNATELY Snoops is eager to cement his reputation as a dedicated cat-chaser . . . BUT, there is a problem. The Brat and Dad are standing in the way.

AND Dad is holding a full tray of free-range eggs.

I remember my mother screaming, and then I must have gone into a state of shock because from then on, my recall of events is somewhat hazy.

Possible Case for the defence of OZZIE DEVON KINGSFORD, who is the great-great-great-great-grandson of a world famous explorer, **and has been charged with:**

1 Wrecking his Mum's kitchen.
2 Destruction of delicious pudding ingredients.
3 Causing irrevocable damage to a tray of eggs.
4 Encouraging Snoops to chase cats.

5 Causing his little sister to fall down the steps and hurt her knee. (Take note — it was actually Snoops that knocked **The Brat** down the steps.)

6 Giving Dad cause to lose his calm-cool-composure.

7 Driving Mother to a state of near-fatal **EXASPERATION**.

 If I had been allowed to go to band practice with Fletch none of these events would have happened.

The time is exactly 11.43 am.

Dad has gone to the supermarket to buy some ready-made puddings — then he will pick up Fletch from band practice and come home via the Free-Range Egg Farm.

The Brat is lying on the couch watching television.

Mum put an ice pack on her knee, and told

her . . . "Just stay here and rest, and do keep your leg propped up."

Having been declared menaces to society, Snoops and I have been banished to my bedroom for the rest of our natural lives.

I was not banished until AFTER I had finished the vacuum cleaning.

I'm lying on my bed contemplating the

meaning of life — the rain is still pouring down, and the wind is making whistling noises — but I'm convinced I can still hear the sound of the forest sprites laughing at my desperately despondent situation.

Course of action: I MUST find out more about these mysterious creatures and discover a way to stop them pestering me for the rest of my living days.

■■◤

Fletch is wearing a silly grin on his face when he comes into my room.

"I've just heard your dad's side of the story," he says.

"I bet you have," I tell him, "but take my word for it, I AM ONCE AGAIN AN INNOCENT VICTIM of an

INJUSTICE — and I wasn't even given a fair trial!"

He laughs, "I bet it was funny, especially your dad losing the eggs!"

I nod my head, "Looking at it from a spectator's point of view, it would have been the laugh of the week, if not the month, or maybe even THE YEAR. But I tell you what — I reckon those forest sprites were hanging around having a laugh at my expense. Maybe they even planned the whole thing for their personal amusement!"

Fletch nods his head in agreement.

"Yeah!" he whispers. "That's what I figured. You've got to give them the Humpty Dumpty, the sooner they fall off the wall the better."

I find myself looking around before replying.

"They could prove to be a serious problem."

"I reckon so," Fletch whispers. "We'll talk about it another time," he points a finger to the window, "when we're away from the sprite-spies."

"Do you think they're listening?" I whisper back.

Fletch nods his head and then says in a loud voice . . .

"Your mum says to tell you that you can come out when your cousins arrive."

"HA!" I say, "I might not want to come out when those geeks arrive; I might prefer to stay here and use my superior intelligence to dwell on the unfairness of the justice system."

AN EEKY GEEKY INVASION

The second bit of this day, Saturday the 15th of December, which is the date that Uncle Rusty arrives.

Weather: it's still raining and the wind has come up even more, in fact, you could say it's blowing a gale.

12.42 pm: Fletch goes looking for some food and then joins me in my bedroom. He brings with him two corned beef, cheese and lettuce sandwiches (one each), and the latest news. "Your mum said to tell you that your

Uncle Rusty rang up and he's at Auckland airport, but there's been a hold-up as his luggage has gone missing, and in his luggage are some very important, confidential papers that relate to the World Bank Investment State of Affairs . . . and worse still, he has also lost all the presents he brought over from Australia — but once he gets the luggage-tracking-devices activated then he will head this way."

He pauses for a bite of his sandwich, "And your mum also said to tell you, that she would have come and told you this news herself, but she's NOT talking to you."

"HUMPH," I grumble, "you can go back and tell her it's a two-way thing, I'm NOT talking to HER either."

We sprawl out on our beds and read *The Weirdo Weekly Wag* magazines.

It's so dark and miserable outside we have to turn the light on; otherwise we will strain our eyes. (For further information on this subject, Google "avoid eye strain".)

Fletch is intensely interested in the article about the pesky forest sprites — while I'm wrapped up in the story about a lost fire-eating tribe that lives deep inside the Santa Ana volcano in El Salvador, when I hear a car pull up our driveway.

The time is exactly 2.18 pm.

I look out the window and I see a red station wagon, and inside are Aunt Nellie, Uncle Andy and the three Geeks. I watch them clamber out of the car and run quickly up the steps . . . Uncle Andy is carrying a big chilly-bin, which I guess contains more

food to feed the multitude.

"HELP! HELP!" I exclaim loudly. "Blow your **bugle** and call up the **cavalry**; it's a treble Geek **invasion**."

███◣

Five minutes later Dad pops his head around my bedroom door.

He shoots a dark-dagger look at me, and his voice is super-grouchy.

"Ozzie, come and introduce Fletch to your cousins," then he points a serious finger at me, **"AND I EXPECT YOU TO BE ON YOUR BEST BEHAVIOUR."**

Fletch and I roll eyes at each other.

 Sometimes life can be a perpetual pain.

We find The Brat
is still stretched
out on the couch
surrounded by
an army of dumb
Barbie dolls.
Cousin Miriam
the Geeky
Mouse is (har!
har!) being
introduced to
each dumb doll one
at a time, which is really boring girl-stuff.

The Brat sees me walk into the room
and she shoots me a mean eye, while Miriam
sneaks a quick look and then narrows her eyes
and turns away. I reckon she's thinking:

yuCCccky0000, here is that

horrible, mean and nasty Ozzie who tried to kill his dear baby sister.

Dad and Uncle Andy have claimed ownership of the television and are watching a game of golf. Dad ignores me — Uncle Andy gives a half-smile and waggles his fingers as a sort-of casual greeting. Aunt Nellie is busy unpacking more food supplies out of a chilly-bin; she gives Fletch and me an amused look and then winks at us.

I wink back, and I can see she's trying not to laugh.

 Sometimes my Aunt Nellie can be nicer than my mother.

Mum walks over, and she stands next to Fletch and makes an announcement:

"Let me introduce you to Fletch Jessup." She smiles and ruffles Fletch's hair and says,

"As well as being Ozzie's **loyal** friend, this young man is considered a part of our family." Then she turns to me and says in an unaffectionate voice, "Ozzie, your cousins have brought a new game to play — it's called *Sixteen Thousand Quiz-able Questions*, would you please go through to the dining room and set up at the table." Then she gives me a terribly false smile, "And I **DO** expect you to look after your guests."

I have long suspected that my parents like Fletch better than me. Now with my mum ruffling

Fletch's hair, which I have recently decided is a sign of motherly affection, I am left inwardly devastated while being forced to maintain an outwardly superhuman exterior.

 I do not recommend playing *Sixteen Thousand Quiz-able Questions*. I RECKON it has to be THE DUMBEST GAME I HAVE ever PLAYED. How am I supposed to know that Woodrow Wilson was the 23rd President of the United States of America? And that The Granite City is a nickname for Aberdeen.

In my opinion, the answer to these questions is of no worth when it comes to

survival in this modern dog-chase-cat world
— and it is ALSO humiliating that the score
sheet reads:

Fletch - 220 pts
Geek 1 - 298 pts
Geek 2 - 235 pts
Ozzie - 65pts
Loser

In case you haven't noticed: Ozzie
Kingsford, who is the first-born Kingsford
male child of this generation, is firmly
established at the bottom of the academic
heap!

AND if my Geeky cousins give me one
more "Ozzie-is-a-born-loser" look, I might

go on the blink
and forget that
at heart I am
a peacekeeper
and **whack
them one.**

 If it wasn't so wet and windy outside,
and if I wasn't so hungry, I might just
consider **running away** from home.

I feel a bit better when at 3.16 pm Aunt Nellie
comes into the dining room carrying a plate of
delectable chocolate cakes.

"Here you are boys," she says "something
to help keep the brain cells ticking over."
She puts the plate down on the table and

says, "Your uncle just rang up again. He's on the motorway out of Auckland, but there's been an accident, they've closed the road and there's so much traffic built up he doesn't know when they'll get moving again."

She sighs, "And your grandparents can't get into town because there are slips and trees down through the gorge, also the river is rising rapidly and the police are advising motorists not to travel today, and they were going to pick up Emma."

"So what are they going to do?" I ask.

"They'll see what happens overnight, and try to get in tomorrow. I only hope they make it as your mother's prepared enough food to feed an army." Then she gives me a big smile, "I hope Rusty gets here okay, you'll enjoy spending time with him — in fact, you remind me of him. My goodness, he was always in trouble as a kid. I remember how he used to spin this **ridiculous** story about how it wasn't really him that caused trouble, that it was a team of forest sprites that followed him home from school camp."

Aunt Nellie laughs — "Har, har!"

The Geeks laugh — "Har, har, har, har!"

But Fletch and I don't laugh — we look at each other with eyes-wide-open.

███◨

5.35 pm: There is another phone call from Uncle Rusty — he is now off the Auckland motorway, but the traffic is being diverted due to flooding. This is going to add another hour to his journey, so we are not to expect him for tea. He's going to grab something along the way because he is so hungry.

Mum rings **the Bothersomes** to
say that Rusty will be late, and Missus
Bothersome says, "Ooops, didn't you get our
message? A sweet little girl answered the
phone; she said she had been left home **all
by herself**, and that she was told to take
messages. I told her we're sorry — we won't

be able to make it today, but we are going to pop in tomorrow."

As we have visitors, Mum is forced to suppress her extreme mortification mixed with EXASPERATION at discovering her dear daughter is an accomplished fibber.

Dad doesn't give two hoots that the invited guests won't be coming for tea.

"Oh well, plenty of food for us!" he announces in a happy tone of voice. "And I'm sooooo hungry . . ."

But maybe he shouldn't have said that, because at that VERY moment there is a gigantic gust of wind, the lights go *flicker-flicker-flicker*, and then the power goes off.

A state of organised panic sets in.

Mum goes, "***Grrrrr*rump***,"** and jams the half-cooked cord-don-blurr chook back in the fridge with all the other stuff she was going to cook, and we have ham, lettuce, tomato and cheese sandwiches for tea. Dad can't find any candles, so we sit with his shed torch shining on us, which Mum says is not very romantic.

Dad grumps that romance has nothing to do with it, and at least we have light.

THEN Uncle Andy questions why we don't have an emergency kit put aside with candles. This questioning makes Dad even grumpier — as our dad is a tyrant at heart, he doesn't like being quizzed about anything, especially by a know-it-all Highly-Respected-Scientific-Big-Wig.

AND, Miriam and Holly don't like each other any more.

Miriam says: Holly punched her, pinched her, and yelled at her.

NOW she's clinging to Aunt Nellie, and bawling her eyes out.

She keeps saying over and over again, "I WANT TO GO HOME!"

Aunt Nellie is comforting Miriam, while giving Holly a fierce look.

Our mum is suffering from further
EXASPERATION because Holly won't
stop grizzling, and grumping that she wants to
watch her favourite television programme and
it's **NOT FAIR** that the power has gone off,
and how she doesn't like Miriam any more and
why doesn't Miriam **GO HOME!**

AND the Geeks are still afflicted with the swollen-head-syndrome, and keep blabbing on about how they beat Fletch and me at sixteen thousand dumbest-ever questions. Fletch keeps looking at me as much to say: how can we escape? And while all this is happening our un-courageous dog Snoops is sitting quivering under the table (just in case there's another big gust of wind).

AND things are getting even more tedious-boring and mind-numbing when the phone rings at exactly 7.47 pm and Uncle Rusty tells us that he's run into more problems . . . the road south is now closed due to flooding, so he's stopped over at a motel and will spend the night there. Upon receiving this news our visitors (who seem eager to escape) pack up their stuff really fastfastfast and go home.

The Brat is then herded off to her room for a lecture on:

A. ANSWERING the PHONE. ✓

B. Telling FIBS. ✓

C. Being UNKIND to MIRIAM. ✓

D. EMBARRASSING her PARENTS.

The power is still off when we go to bed.

The wind is strong-as and is making weirdo whistling noises.

Snoops comes into bed with me and sneaks under the duvet.

I reckon he's still nervous about the wild weather — so I give him a pat to comfort him. He snuggles closer to me and to give him confidence, I tell him he's a brave little fellah.

Fletch says in a quiet, contemplative voice, "Hey, whadda you reckon about your Uncle Rusty and the forest sprites, do you think it could be genetic?"

"What do you mean?"

"Like maybe there's something in your genes that attracts weirdos?"

"I dunno, I've never heard of that," I say. "It's a **horrible thought**, but I guess it could happen."

"You've got to talk to him about the sprites," Fletch says.

"You reckon?" I ask.

"Yeah, you do," Fletch concludes. "Because if he had them, and now he's got rid of them — you've got to find out how he did it," he lowers his voice, "or else you might be stuck with them for **ever** and **ever**."

INTRODUCING RUSTY UNCLE

Sunday the 16th of December, which is nine days before Christmas. Weather: it's stopped raining. There's a bit of sun, and a bit of cloud.

The time is 6.45 am and there's a car horn going toot-hoot-toot, right outside my bedroom window. Snoops automatically starts up his house-protection act and jumps up

at the window going, "Wuff — Ruff — Wuff."

Fletch rolls over in bed and gives me a dormant-dozy look and mumbles, "Jeez, what the heck is making that awful noise."

I pull the curtains, and I see a white car in our driveway, and out of it clambers a tall fellah with a mop of bright red hair. He sees me looking at him and his face breaks out into a smile, then he winks and gives me the thumbs up.

"It's UNCLE RUSTY," I bellow — "He's HERE!"

My bellow wakes up the whole house, and everyone comes out of their bedrooms and rushes to the door — that is, except for Dad, who has a loo-stop along the way.

Har! Har! After Mum not seeing her beloved brother for ten years, the first glimpse

he gets of her is in her old blue dressing gown, with her hair sticking up all over the place — but it really doesn't matter, cos everyone is so excited.

■ ■ ◨

After Mum excuses herself and dashes about making herself look a bit beautiful, we all sit around the table and have breakfast.

Dad sets the toaster up on the table.

Mum makes a pot of tea.

Then Rusty tells us about the adventures of the last few days.

Dad sits there with a silly-sociable-I-am-a-nice-person grin glued on his face, and doesn't even threaten me with instant death when I overload my toast with honey and it d r i b b l e s on the table.

Mum's being soft-gooey and sentimental, and keeps saying, "Oh it's so good to see you," over and over again and giving her brother big cuddles, and then commenting about how much Uncle Rusty looks like her fine-upstanding-only-son (who happens to be me).

 This is a SIGNIFICANT change in attitude from the previous twenty-four hours.

Her rowdiness The Brat is sitting on the chair next to Dad and for some unknown reason is actually being quiet.

I figure Dad has threatened The Brat with expulsion from the human race if she gives our guest the impression she is ill-disciplined. And further more, I reckon this action has been taken to show my parents in a good light.

That is: so it will appear they are accomplished at the task of raising a family.

Snoops is not quite sure about having another
Hot-Head in the house, and he's sitting
next to me giving little anxious shivers.

"Am I going to **like** this **new person?**"
his body language is saying.

I give him a pat and whisper to him to put
on his personality-assessment cap, and I'm

pleased to see that after a minute or three his tail starts a slow wag-wag-wag, which means that Rusty has been declared dog user-friendly.

When Rusty talks, he flaps his hands around like he's talking in sign language.

"It's just been incredible," Rusty is saying while waving his arms about in the air, "one jolly thing after another, fog, rain, lost luggage, it's almost like someone's been trying to stop me getting here!"

"Well, you are here now," says Mum, "and I'd better get on the phone and organise everyone to come around for lunch — shall we say one o'clock?" she questions while looking at Dad.

"Any time that suits you darling," Dad says in a smug voice, "after all, you're the food organiser."

"No dear," Mum says back in an equally smug voice, "seeing the weather has fined up, you can cook on the barbecue."

Dad's face drops . . .

Giving him no time to argue, Mum jumps to her feet . . .

The Brat grabs Rusty's hand and pulls at him.

"Come and see my Barbie dolls," she says in her squawkiest voice. Rusty gives me a sort of apologetic look and departs the room . . . then Dad stands up, "I'd better check out the barbecue," he says in a glum voice, "and seeing you boys haven't got anything better to do, you can clear up the dishes. I think the dishwasher is working okay, but you'd better hang around and keep an eye on it — your mother will do her nut if it floods the kitchen again."

Fletch jumps to his feet and gives a military salute.

"YES SIR, Mister Kingsford, you can rely on me — I promise to put this lazy Ozzie lad step-by-step through my **certified** kitchen training programme."

Dad gives Fletch a questioning look, which plainly says: *Is this youngster making fun of me?*

THINGS HAPPEN

it is now 4.47 pm and the house is full
of people.

Gramma Grace has pulled out the
photo albums, and she keeps sticking them
under everyone's nose going:

"OH! Look at this! OH my goodness!
Do you remember when this was taken?"

Granddad Pete is having a snore-off in
the corner chair. Great-Aunt Emma has
been kidnapped by The Brat and is being
introduced to her army of Barbie dolls.

Aunt Nellie is helping Mum in the kitchen.

Uncle Andy is watching a science programme on the television with the three geeks. It is something to do with the preparation and use of bi-functional molecules related to the DNA sequence — I must say it looks like riveting viewing.

Nigel Bothersome and his wife are swapping life-stories with Rusty.

Dad is playing putt-a-golf-ball around the lawn, but Snoops keeps pinching the golf balls and running off with them while Dad waves his golf club at him, and yells . . . "Bring that ball back here."

But Snoops just tosses his head in the air and laughs his doggy laugh: "Wuffy-ha-

wuffy-ha-wuffy you can't catch me, I am a mean doggy machine, and I've got the ball, and I can run faster than you! Wuffy-ha-wuffy-ha-wuffy."

■■◧

Fletch and I sit and watch Snoops having fun, and I tell Fletch the story about how Dad used to have a putting-machine that you hit golf balls into, and it spat them back out at you — but The Brat jammed the head of one of her dumb Barbie dolls in the hole, and the hair got stuck and it wouldn't come out.

Mum, Dad and I all had turns at tugging and pulling, but the Barbie refused to budge — in the end Dad cut the hair off the doll while The Brat squawked in protest . . . but the machine was never the same again and instead of spitting out golf balls, it spat out bits of Barbie hair.

"Why didn't he get another one?" Fletch asks.

"He did," I say, "but he left it out on the lawn, and I accidentally ran it over with the lawn mower. It made a dreadful clattering noise and jammed up all my blades."

"Jeez," says Fletch, "I bet it did."

"And one day Snoops wasn't looking where he was aiming and did a sloppy poo on the third one, which Mum then declared UNHYGIENIC and threw in the rubbish. Dad was a bit miffed about that one, but Mum reckons if Dad can't put his toys away when he's finished playing with them, then it's his problem."

At the mention of her name Mum magically appears and says, "Fletch, your mother has just rung up, they've arrived home and suggest you should head home and say hello to your Nana."

I help him gather up his things, and then he says to my mum: "Thank you very much for having me to stay."

Mum gives him a big beaming smile, and coos, "Fletch, you are always welcome, you are a trouble-free house guest. Now, do you want a ride home?"

Fletch says, "No, it's okay, I'll walk."

I wander out to the gate with him and before he heads off, he gives me a serious look and says, "You make sure you get some time alone with your uncle to talk about the sprites."

I nod my head, "I will," I tell him.

He gives me the thumbs up and then turns around and walks off up the street.

By the time everyone goes home my wicked watch says the time is 8.47 pm.

Uncle Rusty needs to get some sleep before he heads back to Auckland.

He gives a big yawn.

"I've gotta get some rest." He looks at his watch and does some silent mathematical calculations, "If I'm going to catch that plane, I'll have to be away by four o'clock."

Mum orders him off to have a shower, "And give me your clothes and I'll wash them and put them in the dryer so they are fresh for morning." Then she turns to Dad, "Could you find a pair of pyjamas for Rusty?"

I decide to wait until Rusty comes out of the shower.

But **The Brat** grabs hold of him.

"Come and say goodnight to my Barbie dolls," she pleads, "they like you!"

I wait until he comes out of **The Brat's** bedroom, but Mum grabs him.

"Go to sleep," she says to Holly, and herds Rusty off to see some photos that she took today and has downloaded on to her computer. She spots me loitering and orders, "And you get to bed Ozzie, it's school tomorrow!"

■■◪

It is now 9.38 pm.

Snoops is fast asleep.

He's snoring, and his feet are twitching as if

he's chasing a cat, or some other unfortunate critter. I yawn . . . I wish I was asleep too.

I am so tired, and I have to keep blinking my eyes to keep awake.

If I fall asleep now and miss out on talking to Rusty, the rest of my life could be put in jeopardy. (For further information on this subject, Google "stay awake and live".)

Four minutes later I hear footsteps down the hallway, and peek out the door, only to find Dad has nabbed Rusty and is showing him his Golf Trophies.

Fifteen minutes later I hear Mum and Dad saying, "Goodnight Rusty."

I give it exactly seven more minutes and then I sneak-sneak-sneak out of bed and peep around my door . . . Mum and Dad are just going into their bedroom . . . they shut the door . . . now is my chance.

I sneak down the hallway, and tap on Rusty's bedroom door; he opens it and peers out at me with two bleary eyes.

"I'm sorry, but I need to talk to you," I tell him, putting my fingers to my lips and pointing at my parents' bedroom door. "It's a matter of life and death."

He nods his head and motions for me to come inside.

He flops back on his bed, and I sit next to him.

He smiles, "You remind me of my youth," he tells me.

I nod my head, "I reckon I'll grow up to look just like you."

"You poor kid," he says, "I hope you don't mind?"

"Nah," I reply, "Fletch and I think you're pretty cool."

He reaches out a hand and **ruffles my hair!**

Question: Is ruffling my hair a genetic trait?

I look at him with **serious intent:** "Uncle Rusty," I say, "I need to know, did you have problems with forest sprites when you were my age?"

When I say those words, the expression on his face changes . . .

He frowns.

He looks about the room.

Then he sits up and leans back against the wall.

"**Who** told you about the sprites?" He questions.

"Aunt Nellie," I tell him.

He nods his head, "Yes, she used to tease me about them when I was younger."

"Did my mother tease you too?" I ask.

"No," he says with a smile, "she was too busy playing pretend school teachers and bossing us around. In fact, I reckon you could say she was the **bossiest big sister** in the **whole wide world!**"

I sigh, "So, she hasn't changed much?"

"Not one little bit, and in my opinion, she never will!" We both have a little laugh, and then he asks, "What do you want to know about the sprites for?"

"Because, I've got a problem with sprites too."

"Really?" he asks.

I nod my head, "They latched on to me on my birthday, and I figure they intend to hang around."

He sighs, "Where were you when these sprites found you?"

I tell him about the events of my birthday, how Dad put the car in a ditch, and we were stuck in the Tasman forest block, when we were supposed to be at Cracker Beach.

"Was there a trout fishing spot there?" he questions.

I nod my head.

"Well, this is a coincidence . . . because I think we are talking about the very same spot where the sprites found me. We had a school camp out there . . . this expert fishing guy came along and taught us how to land a trout . . . I remember, there was this strange atmosphere . . ."

"Like somebody or something was laughing at you?" I ask.

"Yes . . . a source of amusement is the way I see it. I've done quite a lot of reading on the subject, and it seems that the sprites are a bunch of comedians, they use us humans the same way as ventriloquists use their dummies."

"So how did you get rid of your sprites?" I ask.

He slowly shakes his head, "What makes you think I got rid of them?"

"DO YOU MEAN THEY ARE STILL WITH YOU?" My voice comes out sounding louder than I meant it to . . .

"Shhh," goes Rusty, "don't wake the house . . . and yes, they are still with me. Why do you think I lose my luggage, why do I get held up on motorways, fogged in at airports, and who do you think brought this rain that's flooded half the country?"

"I never thought of that," I tell him.

He smiles, "In the course of my investigations I discovered our forest sprites are directly related to the Irish Leprechaun. It is said, that way back in history, a group of the little people set off to have an adventure and they stowed away on a sailing ship that brought the early immigrants to this country. However, on their arrival they found, unlike their homeland, there were no big bustling cities to live in. Nevertheless, being adaptable creatures, they stayed and made homes in the native bush, and, when the settlers cleared the bush, they moved into man-made forests where they remain to this very day. And Ozzie, I also learned that once the sprites have adopted people as objects of amusement, they don't let them go."

"So what can I do?" I question.

"I'm sorry to say my young friend, but all you can do is grin and bear it," he says, "and I suggest when you grow up you get a safe

indoor job
— I wanted to
be an airline
pilot, or
perhaps join
the air force and
fly jet-fighters
. . . but can you imagine
what mischief a bunch of flying-high sprites
could come up with?"

He puts on a glum face, "So that is why I
settled for a job in banking. Life is not easy
when you have a team of playful characters
tagging along behind."

I give a big-sad-sigh and nod my head,
"Why do they follow us, and not somebody
else?"

"I don't know Ozzie, maybe we possess a
certain characteristic, or perhaps they just

like redheads," he says with a laugh. Then he puts his hand out and once again ruffles my hair, "But take my word for it, they will never deliberately hurt you, they simply want to play, and I can guarantee you one thing, with a pack of sprites around, your life is going to be **really-really-really** interesting."

EXTRAORDINARY STUFF

monday the 17th of December, which is eight days before Christmas.

Weather: hot and sunny.

I wake up when I hear a car motor start . . .

"Oh no," I say to myself, "Uncle Rusty must be leaving."

I jump out of bed and run as fast as I can, but by the time I get to the back door, the car is going up the road.

Mum is standing in the doorway having a

soppy cry in her hanky.

I walk up to her, and take hold of her arm and give her a little pit-pat.

"I like your brother," I say.

She looks at me and gives a watery smile . . .

"Thank you," she says, "I like him too."

Then she puts her hand in her dressing gown pocket and brings out a golden chain with a medallion attached.

"He said this is for you, and to say that he ever-so-much enjoyed your company," she blows her nose, "and that you have a **special bond**." And with those words she promptly bursts back into soppy sobbing . . .

I look hard at the medallion, and there enclosed in the golden circle, are two **real wicked-looking** dragons, which are either having a fight, or are all tangled up.

Fletch is waiting for me at the corner, and we walk to school together. I tell him about my talk with Uncle Rusty, and show him the medallion.

He looks at it with serious eyes and then declares, "This is an ancient Chinese good luck charm, and I reckon it's made of **real** gold."

He looks hard at it again, "Or maybe **fool's gold**, or bronze, or some sort of copper-plating. But, I reckon you'd better keep it around your neck at all times or it might get nicked. Whatever it's made of it looks valuable to me."

"Wicked stuff," I say, while tucking the dragons down my shirt.

"And I've been giving this sprite business some historic consideration," Fletch says in a contemplative tone of voice, "and as far as we know, at this present time there are only two of you in this whole-big world that the forest sprites find to be worthy of absolute devotion."

"DEVOTION," I say while tossing the thought around in my brain, "I hadn't quite thought of it like that."

"Why else would the critters want to leave their natural habitat? You have to face the fact that you must possess a magnetism that they can't resist." He points a finger right at my middle bits and exclaims, "They want to be with you — it's not their fault they are by nature mischievous, troublesome and somewhat catastrophic."

"You reckon so?" I question.

"Yep."

"So that makes me sort of EXTRAORDINARY?"

"Yep, it sure does."

"I've never been considered **EXTRAORDINARY** before," I say, while puffing my chest out with pride. "Do you reckon they'd do an article about me in *The Weirdo Weekly Wag*?"

He nods his head and rolls his eyeballs at me . . .

"Yes, you are definitely extraordinarily-weirdo enough for that."

Then he gives a curtsey like a girl would when she was meeting the Queen and says in a posh voice: "Oh mighty, weirdest-one, please may I carry your school bag for you?"

When he says those words a raging-roaring wind rushes past.

The trees in people's gardens thrash about.

Washing is whipped off clotheslines . . .

The lady who is walking in front of us says a bleep word when her hat blows off.

An ice cream sign blows over by the corner shop.

Up ahead there's a man unloading advertising pamphlets from a van. He watches in amazement as a mini whirl-wind sweeps by and picks up (by my rapid calculation) the eighteen-and-a-half-thousand,

three-hundred-and-forty-seven pieces
of colourful paper and whisks them forever
upwards into the stratosphere — then, after
the mini whirl-wind jumbles and twists them
about, they slowly twirl back to earth.

 It is a spectacular sight and people
stop in the street and stare upward.

I hear the pamphlet man say, "What the
bleepity-bleep was that?"
While in the distance there is laughter.
"Har! Har! Har! Har!"
Fletch and I look at each other . . .
"Did you hear that?" I ask.
He nods his head . . .
"Uncle Rusty did say life would be
interesting," I tell him.
"**Radical stuff**," says Fletch, "I've never
seen it rain paper before."

Then we roll our eyeballs . . . and join the sprites in somewhat half-witted, happy, hysterical hilarity.

COMING SOON.

An Electrifying New Year in the Life of Ozzie Kingsford

It's school holiday time and Ozzie and his mate Fletch are rounding up equipment for a specialised scientific experiment — while at the same time, trying to avoid a dose of the dreaded 'juvenile overwork syndrome'.

UNFORTUNATELY Dad gets donged on the head by a wayward golf ball; which causes Mum to suffer from extreme **exasperation** – whilst young sister Holly (alias **The Brat**), and the pesky forest sprites continue to make double-trouble for our unlikely heroes.

LOOK OUT FOR MORE TITLES IN THE OZZIE KINGSFORD SERIES!

A Shark Tooth Bay Holiday in the Life of Ozzie Kingsford

Back to School Days in the Life of Ozzie Kingsford

ABOUT THE AUTHOR

Val Bird spent her childhood years in Hastings, before settling in the seaside town of Whakatane — where she lives in a nice quiet house, with husband Ros, two big hairy dogs (Fudge and Wally) and a crazy, bed-hogging, tabby cat called Candy-kit.

One day her daughter Rebecca asked Val to write a children's book that she could illustrate. At the time Val thought, "Oh my giddiness, can I do that?" And yes, it turned out (after a few false starts) that indeed she could, and that's how Ozzie Kingsford and his entertaining family came to life.

Val would like to thank Random House for recognising Ozzie's potential, and hopes in the future you (the reader) will enjoy further adventures with the Kingsford family.

About the Illustrator

Born in Hastings, raised in Whakatane, and now residing in Hamilton, Rebecca Cundy is married to Troy, and lives in a very happy house. When not working, or mothering daughters Hannah and Brooklyn, she spends her time tending to the needs of three cute cats (Chance, Pebbles and Nugget) and Bentley the Big Handsome Boxer (even though, secretly, sometimes she would rather be off riding her motorbike). As a child Rebecca spent hours and hours drawing cartoon characters, which started her off on a pathway to graphic design. Now, aged 37, she is delighted to call herself a Children's Book Illustrator. Yes, dreams combined with hard work do come true. Rebecca hopes you will enjoy the Kingsford family characters as much as she enjoyed creating them.